Hasan's Idea

by Jill Atkins and José Rubert

W
FRANKLIN WATTS

Hasan's Idea

Contents

Chapter 1

Getting Ready for Christmas

It was getting dark as Hasan Rashid hurried home from school. It would soon be time for the school holidays to start. As he walked, he glanced up at the colourful street decorations. Everyone was getting ready for Christmas.

At school, he and his friends had talked about what they were going to do in the school holidays. As Hasan walked past the brightly lit shops, he thought about the lesson they had had with Ms Fisher that afternoon.

"We have been thinking about food as our topic this term," said Ms Fisher. "Talk in groups about the food you eat on special occasions when you celebrate with your family and friends."

Hasan worked with his friends James, Rowan, Holly, Devi and Ellie. "You go first, Devi," said James. Devi told everyone about the food her family ate together at Diwali – the spicy samosas, and delicious, sticky sweets like *laddoos* and *barfi*. The children all licked their lips.

"Your turn, Hasan," said James.

"Well," said Hasan, thinking. "At Eid al-Fitr, we have a big celebration with lots of food. It comes at the end of the month of Ramadan. That's the sacred time of fasting and prayer."

"Oh yes," said Ellie. "That's when people don't eat during the day, isn't it?"

"That's right," said Hasan. "From sunrise to sunset every day. Then, at the end of Ramadan, we celebrate the holy day of Eid. This is a special day for Muslims. In my family, we all gather together and everyone brings food and we have a huge feast. It's wonderful."

"That's interesting, Hasan," said James. "I didn't know about fasting. I'd like to know more about that. Now, what about your special food, Ellie?"

Ellie explained that she was looking forward to Christmas dinner. "We eat turkey and stuffing and roast potatoes. Nan brings Christmas cake. Grandad eats so much that he falls asleep and snores!"

All the children laughed.

As Hasan arrived home, a delicious spicy aroma wafted around him. It was coming from the kitchen. His teenage sister, Amira, was already sitting at the table.

"I'm starving!" she said.

"Time to eat, Hasan," called Mum. "Get washed and sit down ready for dinner."

At that moment, Dad came home from work.

He ruffled Hasan's hair. "Had a good day?" he asked.

Hasan nodded. "It was really interesting," he said, "and it has made me think."

"What about?" asked Dad.

"Well," said Hasan, "we were talking about how everyone does different things and eats different things when we have our celebrations.

"My friends really wanted to find out about Ramadan and why people fast. I'd like to tell them some more about it. Could you help me think about what to say?"

"Let's eat first," said Dad, "and then we'll talk about Ramadan while we clear up after dinner."

Chapter 2

Hasan Explains

Next morning, Hasan met his friends, James and Ellie, at the school gate.

"You know what we were talking about yesterday?" said Ellie. "Well, I was wondering, aren't Muslims allowed to eat anything at all during the day when it's Ramadan?"

Hasan shook his head. "No," he said. "When Mum and Dad are fasting, they don't eat anything between dawn and dusk. I talked about it with my dad last night."

Holly, Rowan and Devi joined in the conversation.

"How long does Ramadan last?" asked Devi.

"A month," said Hasan.

"A whole month!" said Holly, with a gasp. "That's a long time! So what else do you do during Ramadan?"

Hasan could see that they were interested so he kept on talking.

"So, my parents really look forward to Ramadan," he said. "You might think that they don't like fasting, but that's not true."

"My parents get up very early, before dawn, to eat," he explained. "This meal is called *suhoor*. It's like breakfast, only they eat quite a lot because they won't eat for the rest of the day, until dusk.

"Then we have a big evening meal with the whole family together."

"We have a big meal to celebrate Diwali," said Devi. "We're Hindu. We have a big party at the end of October."

"Oh yes, I remember," said Rowan. "Mum and I came to the party, didn't we? You called it the Festival of Light."

Devi grinned. "Yeah. We dress up in bright clothes and have lovely food and lights and fireworks."

"Your party was great!" said Rowan.

At that moment, the bell went for class to begin.

It was the last day of term and everyone was in

a party mood. The children played games,

ate sweets and sang songs with Ms Fisher.

As the school day ended, everyone rushed

towards the gates, hurrying to get home.

"Happy Christmas! See you in January!"

shouted Ellie and James.

Devi slapped Hasan on the back.

"Enjoy your holiday!" she said with a grin.

Hasan laughed. "Yeah! And you, too!"

Chapter 3

Christmas Holidays

The school holidays were wonderful, but the days seemed to last forever. Hasan missed playing with his classmates, especially James. He wondered what they were doing with their families.

One day, Hasan and Amira went to visit their aunt and uncle. Later, as they hurried home in the cold December air, they heard music and saw people coming out of a church.

"Oh yes," said Hasan. "Today is Christmas Day. Some of my school friends will have presents. I hope they're having a wonderful time."

"I'm sure they are," said Amira. "You'll hear all about it when you go back to school."

"I can't wait to hear if Ellie's grandad fell asleep again this year!" said Hasan, smiling.

A few flakes of snow whirled in the air
and they pulled their coats tighter.

"I've had an idea," said Amira.

"Oh dear," Hasan groaned. He had heard his sister's
ideas before!

"Why not invite your friends to Eid al-Fitr when
it comes?"

Hasan stopped and stared at his sister. Then
he shook his head. "I'm not sure," he said.
"It's a time for families, isn't it?"

Amira linked her arm through his. "Yes, but it's also a time for friends. Why don't you ask Mum and Dad this evening? I'm sure they would be thrilled to have your friends share Eid with us."

Hasan nodded. The more he thought about Amira's suggestion, the more he liked it.

They could find out all about Eid for themselves.

Hasan's stomach did a somersault he was so excited.

It would be wonderful if his friends could come.

As soon as they entered the hallway,

Amira nudged her brother.

"Go on," she whispered. "If you don't even ask ..."

"... I'll never know," finished Hasan, grinning at her.

"Wish me luck!"

Hasan went into the living room.

His mum looked up from her laptop in surprise.

"Hello," she said. "What have you two been planning?"

"Nothing."

"I don't believe you," Mum smiled. "Come on.

Out with it!"

Hasan took a deep breath. As Amira had said, if you don't ask ...

"Well, I was thinking about my friends in school," he said. "You know how we all celebrate different things. Devi is Hindu, and she celebrates Diwali. And today is Christmas Day for Rowan, Ellie, Holly and James. Did you know?"

"Yes, of course," said Mum.

"And we celebrate Eid at the end of Ramadan," said Hasan.

"So?" His mum's smile gave him confidence.

"Well, some of my friends were asking me about Ramadan. They were really interested and I was wondering if I could invite them to our Eid celebrations in the summer?"

"I see."

The door opened and Amira walked into the living room.

"It was my idea, Mum," she admitted.

"I think it's a fantastic idea," said Mum.

"Really?" Hasan beamed at her.

Then, when Dad got home, Hasan told him about Amira's idea.

"I don't see why not," said Dad. "That's a really good idea."

Hassan was thrilled!

He couldn't wait to tell his friends.

Chapter 4

Getting Ready for Eid

A few months later, it was time for Ramadan to begin. When it fell in the summer, it was a long time between dawn and dusk when Hasan's parents would break the day's fast.

Eid al-Fitr would come 30 days after Ramadan began, on the night when the new moon could be seen in the sky. Hasan got more and more excited as the time for the big celebration got closer. He wrote out five invitations:

Hasan Rashid and his family invite you to celebrate Eid al-Fitr with them on Saturday 5th June at 2pm.

Hasan posted one to each of his friends.

"I hope they can come," he said to Amira as they walked home from the postbox.

He didn't have long to wait to find out.

On Monday, as he arrived outside school, four smiling faces greeted him.

"You bet I'll come!" said Devi.

"My dad says I can come, too," said Holly.

"Same with me," said James.

"Me too," said Rowan.

Then Ellie came running across the playing field. Hasan could see her big grin even though she was out of breath. She was waving her invitation.

"Count me in!" she laughed. "This is the coolest thing ever!"

The Eid party was a great success. Everyone wore their best clothes and all the children were given presents. The food was delicious, especially the sweet desserts – sticky baklava, dates, and thick, milky *falooda*.

Hasan went over to talk with his friends. "This is such a cool party," said Rowan.

26

"And there's so much lovely food," gasped Holly.

"I'm full to bursting!" said Devi.

James nodded. He had too much of a mouthful to speak.

"These cakes are awesome!" laughed Ellie. "I wish my mum could taste them. Perhaps she would make some of them at home."

And that was what gave Hasan his fantastic idea.

At school on the following Monday, Hasan told his friends about his idea. They all agreed it was the best brainwave yet, and when Ms Fisher heard about the Eid party, she agreed, too.

So three weeks later, Hasan's class held a 'Sharing Foods Day' for all the parents. Ms Fisher had helped arrange it, but most of the work had been done by the six friends.

Tables were laden with food from the children's different cultures: Christian, Muslim, Hindu, Jewish, Sikh and Buddhist. In turn, the children talked to everyone about how the food was made and explained how they celebrated their different festivals.

"Today was just great," said James as the friends cleared up at the end of the afternoon. "We've learned such a lot about each other and how we celebrate. Hasan, you had the best idea ever. Thank you."

Hasan felt warm inside. "You all helped, too. Together, we make a great team," he grinned. And everyone agreed.

Things to think about

1. What special occasions do you celebrate? This might be a birthday or a celebration in your town.
2. How do you celebrate? Do you have special food for your festival, like the friends in this story?
3. What do you think Hasan, James and the other friends enjoy most about their Sharing Day?
4. If you could have a Sharing Day at your school, what would you most like to find out about your classmates?

Write it yourself

One of the themes in this story is friendship. Now try to write your own story with a similar theme.

Plan your story before you begin to write it.

Start off with a story map:

• a beginning to introduce the characters and where and when your story is set (the setting);

• a problem which the main characters will need to fix in the story;

• an ending where the problems are resolved.

Get writing! Try to use interesting descriptions, such as delicious, sticky sweets; cold December air; flakes of snow whirled in the air, to describe your story world to your reader.

Notes for parents and carers

Independent reading
The aim of independent reading is to read this book with ease. This series is designed to provide an opportunity for your child to read for pleasure and enjoyment. These notes are written for you to help your child make the most of this book.

About the book
Hasan's class have been talking about food for different celebrations, and his friends want to find out more about Eid al-Fitr. Hasan comes up with a great plan to explain all about the festival.

Before reading
Ask your child why they have selected this book. Look at the title and blurb together. What do they think it will be about? Do they think they will like it?

During reading
Encourage your child to read independently. If they get stuck on a longer word, remind them that they can find syllable chunks that can be sounded out from left to right. They can also read on in the sentence and think about what would make sense.

After reading
Support comprehension by talking about the story. What happened?
Then help your child think about the messages in the book that go beyond the story, using the questions on the page opposite. Give your child a chance to respond to the story, asking:
Did you enjoy the story and why? Who was your favourite character?
What was your favourite part? What did you expect to happen at the end?

Franklin Watts
First published in Great Britain in 2019
by The Watts Publishing Group

Series Editors: Jackie Hamley and Melanie Palmer
Series Advisors: Dr Sue Bodman and Glen Franklin
Series Designer: Peter Scoulding
Consultant: Dr Shahrul Hussain

A CIP catalogue record for this book is
available from the British Library.

ISBN 978 1 4451 6509 7 (hbk)
ISBN 978 1 4451 6510 3 (pbk)
ISBN 978 1 4451 6839 5 (library ebook)

Printed in China

Franklin Watts
An imprint of
Hachette Children's Group
Part of The Watts Publishing Group
Carmelite House
50 Victoria Embankment
London EC4Y 0DZ

An Hachette UK Company
www.hachette.co.uk

www.franklinwatts.co.uk

FSC
www.fsc.org
MIX
Paper from
responsible sources
FSC® C104740